APR - - 2022

D1158173

For Loutchitchi
and Zélicorne,
my two princesses.
Mickaël El Fathi

For Lily and Paz.
Charlotte Molas

Charlotte and Mickaël
would like to thank
SNCF, the French railway
company, for the 8534
train that left Hendaye
(right down in the very
south of France, close
to the border with
Spain) at 9:29 am on 28
November 2018 heading
for Paris, which allowed
for an unlikely encounter
between our illustrator
and our author. Sat in
seats 65 and 66, they
began to talk, and,
without that train, this
book might never have
seen the light of day . . .

HARD TIMES
FOR
UNICORN

Mickaël El Fathi
& Charlotte Molas

One day, a young explorer from Siberia
caught the rarest of creatures, a unicorn!

But she lost her the very next day
in a game of cards!

The unicorn was won by a fisherman, who quickly put her to work in the freezing waters of the far north . . .

but the unicorn caught a bad cold and always felt seasick . . . she wasn't a natural at fishing!

At the very next harbour, she was sold to a knight who was very keen on old-fashioned duels. But after an embarrassing defeat, he hastened to pass on the unicorn . . .

. . . to an athlete to use as a vaulting pole.

"Hurrah!" the crowd cheered, and together
they won every trophy.

The unicorn was a worldwide hit!

But then one day, tragedy struck!

A cunning robber, seeing the unicorn's great potential, whisked her away from the athlete.

A few weeks later, the fool was arrested while trying to open a safe.

The police, not quite knowing what to do with the unicorn, dropped her off at a nearby circus, where every Saturday she would perform the "unicorn cannon ball".

But as cinemas and television took over
audiences began to leave the big top.
The ringmaster gave the unicorn to a
cheerful chap who set her to work as
a new attraction at his fun fair.

On the last day of the fun fair, the owner
offered the unicorn to the very last visitor,
who happened to be a boy called Kevin,
who sadly preferred football to pets.

Kevin installed the unicorn on the roof, where she weathered thunder and lightning alongside the TV antenna! This wasn't any fun! She couldn't even see the screen from up there and she got awfully wet when it rained, until one day . . .

. . . some roof workers came to repair
the chimney. They took her with them –
what a headache that turned out to be!

With her horn polished to a shine,
the unicorn found herself with an old
antiques dealer, who told her she'd
make the most elegant coat rack.

That is where I met her. I went in to
buy a carpet and left with a unicorn!
What on earth was I supposed to do
with her?

We hopped aboard the Trans-Siberian Express train and I said goodbye to the unicorn at the gates of the snowy forest. She gave me a kiss and bounded off into the infinite depths of the trees.

Happy and free once again,
at last.

English edition first published 2021 by order of
the Tate Trustees by Tate Publishing, a division of
Tate Enterprises Ltd, Millbank, London SW1P 4RG
www.tate.org.uk/publishing

First published in French as *SALE TEMPS POUR
LES LICORNES*

Original text and illustrations © 2020, Éditions
L'Agrume, Sejer

Translation © 2020, Gilberte Bourget

A catalogue record for this book is available from
the British Library

ISBN 978 1 84976 742 2

Distributed in the United States and Canada by
ABRAMS, New York

Library of Congress Control Number applied for

Printed and bound in China by C&C Offset Printing
Co., Ltd